Who Burned the Hartley House?

Who Burned the Hartley House?

Carole Smith
Illustrated by Glenn Dickson

ALBERT WHITMAN & COMPANY, NILES, ILLINOIS

For Mom, Lois Smith

Library of Congress Cataloging in Publication Data

Smith, Carole.
  Who burned the Hartley house?

  Summary: When a deserted house mysteriously burns,
Larry suspects that a kidnapped boy was held prisoner
there.
    1. Children's stories, American. [1. Mystery and
detective stories] I. Dickson, Glenn, ill. II. Title.
PZ7.S6436Wh   1985   [Fic]   85-682
ISBN 0-8075-8993-4 (lib. bdg.)

The text of this book is printed in twelve-point Times Roman.

Text © 1985 by Carole Smith.
Illustrations © 1985 by Albert Whitman & Company.
Published in 1985 by Albert Whitman & Company, Niles, Illinois.
Published simultaneously in Canada by General Publishing, Limited, Toronto.
All rights reserved. Printed in the United States of America.
10 9 8 7 6 5 4 3 2 1

Contents

1. *The Broken Window*

Larry Kenniston pulled his motorcycle over to the edge of the dirt trail beside the road. He took off his helmet and wiped his damp forehead with the sleeve of his windbreaker.

"Why now?" he asked himself out loud. "Why a flat tire now?"

He stared dismally across the freshly plowed fields, so different from the neatly arranged houses in his neighborhood. It was going to be a long walk home, pushing the bike all the way.

David Wallace, the boy next door, always said nobody should ride alone. Of course, David claimed it was embarrassing to be alone because people thought you didn't have any friends. Maybe David's advice was good—even though his reason was dumb. Larry wished he had a friend who could go for help.

On this first good Saturday of spring, Larry had taken off for a short ride but had ridden farther than he'd intended. Now he was sorry he hadn't waited for David.

Larry checked his watch. It was already a quarter to four, and the family was supposed to leave for his cousin's wedding at five. He'd never make it back in time. Maybe he could telephone and get his dad to pick him up.

Huge pine trees bordered the far edge of the closest field. There might be a house behind those trees.

Larry placed his disabled motorcycle on its stand and started for the trees at a jog. As he ran, he took off his new red helmet and slung it over his arm so it dangled like a padded sand bucket.

If there was no house, he'd have to start walking. Man, if he was late, his mother would scream again about how they should never have let him get that motorcycle.

She kept saying he was too young to be responsible for such a dangerous toy. Whenever anything went wrong, that was the cry. Next came, "Get rid of the bike!" Well, she'd really get after him this time. Because he was too young for a license, he couldn't ride on the street. He could only ride on the trails and the practice field the guys had set up near home. He wasn't supposed to ride nearly as far as he had.

Larry passed the tall pines. Crouched in the shadows behind them was a small two-story house with gray shingles. Some of the shingles were lying in the yard. The doors and windows were framed in dark green wood, the paint peeling. Behind the house, at the end of the drive, was an unpainted shed.

Larry hesitated. The house looked like it might be deserted, but he could see telephone wires. There must be a phone inside, and that was all he needed.

Because he was desperate, Larry marched bravely up the long drive. The helmet on his arm began to worry him. Some people disliked motorcycles and their riders.

In an instant he'd tucked the helmet out of sight under a low bush. Then he continued all the way to the side door, rapped gently, and waited.

Nobody answered.

Larry knocked harder.

Still nothing happened.

Larry slipped around the corner to the front door. But when he rang the bell, no one answered there, either.

Larry turned back toward the first door. As he passed along the side of the house again, he stopped and tried to peer inside. Chips of dark green paint crumbled onto his fingers as he held the windowsill to pull himself higher.

Somebody *did* live in the house. A table with dishes stood just below the window. Through the crack between the drawn curtains, he could see two plates. One had a mug beside it, and near the other was a half-filled glass of milk.

Somebody had to be home. Two people had been eating just a few minutes before.

Larry ran back to the side door. He'd knock as loudly as he could. This time they'd hear him.

Somehow, he stumbled on the low doorstep. He lost his balance, fell forward, and hit the door frame with his shoulder. The hand he'd raised to knock smashed against the low-set six-paned window in the door.

Glass shattered, tinkling onto the small cement porch.

"Oh, no!" Larry groaned. He looked at his hand, expecting to see blood gush out. A red scrape showed across his knuckles, but he wasn't really cut. If only the window had survived as well!

What could he do? He remembered his father had once skidded their station wagon into a parked car. Dad had left a note with his name and address on the driver's seat, and the man had called him later.

Should he leave a note? If he did, he'd have to find paper and pencil. That meant going inside.

Certain the door would be locked, Larry turned the knob. To his amazement, the door opened.

He took a fearful step forward. The kitchen seemed strange and forbidding in the dim light. His heart was pounding frantically.

Small chunks of glass and one fat white seed were scattered on the worn black-and-white floor tiles. Larry brushed at them with his foot. As he did, he noticed an odd smell. It was rotten, like the inside of a garbage can.

Larry moved farther into the room. A frying pan filled with scrambled eggs sat on the front burner of an old stove. The burner was off, but the food had been cooked once. The browned edges of the eggs curled, and the spoiling center had turned green.

On the back burner was a pan filled with a dark liquid that looked like coffee. A film had formed on its top. This burner wasn't turned on, either.

He walked over to an old wooden table. It was chipped and scratched and dirty. His mother wouldn't have liked that table. She would have put a tablecloth on it, and maybe some flowers. Although the room was clean, whoever lived in this house hadn't bothered to make anything look nice.

A wooden chair stood at the table near a plate and glass. Another chair was lying on the floor nearby. Next to it lay a blue airline bag.

The bag seemed interesting, and Larry bent to look inside. He was disappointed to see only crumpled pieces of newspaper. Smoothing one out, he read the headline: "Blaine Sentenced to Jail." Who's Blaine? he wondered. And then, Who cares?

Crumpling the paper again, he stuffed it back into the bag. His hand brushed against the zipper where it was torn loose for about an inch.

Larry reached for another clipping. This one read, "Third Week of Blaine Trial. Survivor to Testify." That sounded more exciting. If he'd been a good reader, he would have found out about this Blaine. Since he didn't read much, he threw the second clipping back.

A corner of gray-green showed at the bottom of the bag. This object was different. Larry grabbed it.

He held up a fragment of stiff paper in amazement. It was money! At the top were the letters *ERICA*, a curly mark, and *100* written in shaded figures. It was almost one-third of a hundred-dollar bill!

Larry had never seen a hundred-dollar bill before.

He set the fragment aside and looked for the rest. Nothing else was in the bag except clippings.

He moved on to pick up the glass of milk. Its sour smell made his nose twitch. Larry whistled a single low note of surprise and set it down quickly.

His whistle sounded shrill in the silent house. The quiet gave him a creepy feeling.

Reaching into his pocket, Larry found a dollar bill, the only money he had, and dropped it onto the table. That should be enough to buy a new windowpane. He didn't see a pencil, so he couldn't write a note.

The things he found were making him uneasy, and he knew now he'd never get home on time. But because this strange house made him curious, he walked toward the arched doorway that led to another room.

A floor board creaked beneath his foot as his weight settled. Except for his own whistle, it was the only sound he'd heard in the house.

The room he found was a mess. A big roll-top desk was piled with magazines, while old clothes littered the floor. Stuffing popped out of a low green chair that faced a television. On the wall was a big calendar with the page turned to August, three years before.

Because the green curtains at the windows were closed, no light could enter the room. If the bulb dangling by a cord from the ceiling hadn't been turned on, he couldn't have seen a thing.

He headed back to the kitchen, moving with increasing fear and speed. Just when the people in this house had been ready to eat, they'd gone away. They'd turned out the kitchen light. But they were in such a hurry that they forgot the light in the second room. The place looked like a scene from one of those movies where the creatures had come from outer space and kidnapped humans.

When he thought of creatures, Larry couldn't help looking over his shoulder. Nothing was there, but suddenly a shrill buzzing sound started and stopped.

He jumped. The noise began and stopped again.

Was that a telephone? It couldn't be, but somewhere in this deserted house a phone was ringing. He didn't want to look for it. All he wanted was to leave the house and forget he'd ever been there.

The telephone stopped ringing, and the silence seemed even more eerie than it had before. Larry rushed out the door, pausing only to slam it, and raced wildly down the drive.

2. Second Visit

After he got home, Larry was rather proud of himself for having explored the empty house alone. He couldn't wait to tell his friend David about it. This was the kind of adventure David loved.

There was no school the next week because of spring vacation. Larry was grounded for making the family late to the wedding, even though he'd ruined an inner tube by riding slowly until he reached a house where he could call his father. Wasn't that enough punishment? His parents were so mad that he never got around to telling about the deserted house.

He would have told his other friends, too, but because he was grounded, he didn't see anyone but David. It rained every day, so he and David overhauled their motorcycles in Larry's garage.

David was athletic and smart and involved with the popular kids at school. Most of the guys he hung out with lived in the same subdivision as Larry and David. These boys all rode bikes and practiced on what they called the Field, several acres of vacant land at the end of Larry's street. The owner of the Field, Mr. Abbott, was waiting to sell to a developer for a good price, and he'd given the neighborhood boys permission to ride there. They had arranged a simple course, and they spent their spare time practicing on it.

To keep up with this crowd, David had pestered his parents until he got a bike. And Larry had demanded one because David had one. With the bikes, they were part of the action. David was already a leader. Larry, more quiet, wasn't noticed much.

"You really know your way around motors," David said as he watched Larry at work on the second day of vacation. "We should get some of the other guys over here so you could help them." He snickered. "Too bad you're not this good at English. Have you told your parents yet that you're failing?"

Larry wiped his hands and stared at a spot of grease on the garage floor. He'd almost forgotten that mid-semester grade.

"I never thought you'd have the nerve to throw

away the letter they sent," David said. He sounded almost admiring. "Lucky the school hasn't called."

"I'm not really failing," Larry explained, wanting to believe that himself. "It was their dumb reading unit that got me in trouble. I'll have the grade up before school's out. I can do most of the rest of the stuff."

"You're going to have to," David warned. "Next time you might not get to the mail first. Then your parents will see the notice for sure."

Larry picked up his chain and wiped it with the rag he'd used on his hands. "Let's work on the bikes," was all he said.

But he didn't stop thinking about that English grade. Why couldn't he pay attention when he was supposed to read a book? Why did the letters always seem to blur so that he couldn't read, even when he wanted to?

Any time he was around machinery, he was alert. Machines never blurred. He could tell as soon as a motor was turned on if it was running well. Taking machines apart and fixing them was what he liked best. When he worked with something mechanical, he paid attention and felt in control. But in school he muddled through most things.

Larry gazed at the rain pouring down outside the

17

open door. If it didn't stop soon, the Field would be a lake, and they couldn't ride for ages. He was a good rider. When he sped across the Field with the wind in his face, he forgot his problems. He'd learned to turn suddenly in a spray of dirt and pebbles. He could rise on a low jump and float through the air for a brief, exciting moment. Who needed English?

"You're getting more gutsy," David said, "and that's a good way to get along with the guys. If you keep improving, you'll be one of our best riders. The way you dumped the letter about your grades was great. And exploring that empty house is your best move yet. Hey, before you tell anyone else about it, let's go back there together."

"I said I didn't want to." Larry dropped his chain, which cascaded noisily against the garage floor.

"Well, you shouldn't have told me about it if you didn't want to go back," David protested. "The whole thing sounds weird, and I want to see it. I want to know why the phone rang when you didn't see any phone."

"That *was* scary," Larry agreed. "The phone wasn't on the desk, or any place where a phone should be. But it sounded like it was real near me. I figure it must have been under those old clothes."

"Did you tell me about those?" David asked.

"They were on the floor in the room with the TV. I think there was a gray shirt and a pair of pants the same color."

"Just an old shirt and pants?" David sounded disappointed.

"I wish now I'd taken a better look at everything," Larry confessed. "But it was spooky being all alone in that house. Why did those people leave without eating? How long had they been gone?"

He shook his head and began to replace the motorcycle chain.

David set his carburetor aside and leaned forward eagerly. "Let's go see if anyone's come back."

"Then you'll want to look through the window," Larry said. That was what he kept thinking about himself. "That's okay, I guess—if nobody's around. But we can't go inside."

"It's no big deal to look in a window," David argued. "What's the matter? Afraid somebody might jump out and grab us?"

Larry laughed, although that was just what he *had* been thinking. "Why would I worry about that? That's kidnapping. Nobody would kidnap big boys like us."

"They do, too, kidnap boys our age," David protested. "My mom and dad were talking last night about a boy who was kidnapped. He doesn't live in Meadowvale, but his uncle works with my dad. And now my mom is afraid to let me out of her sight. But my dad said she had to, that I'd be all right."

"Nobody would want you," Larry teased. "What happened to that boy?"

David sat back and crossed his legs. "He was gone four days. His parents had to pay an enormous ransom. I guess his kidnapper wouldn't still be around looking for anybody else to grab." David sounded sorry there would be no kidnapper to look for.

"Why not?" Larry couldn't always keep up with the way David's mind jumped.

"Because they paid him a big ransom," David explained. "What would you do if you had thousands and thousands of dollars of ransom money? You'd go off and blow it, that's what. Man, just think of all you could do and the places you could go."

Imagining what they could do with a million dollars took up the rest of their afternoon. On Wednesday and Thursday they finished overhauling the bikes. Although the rain still dripped on Friday, David disappeared with his football friends. But on Saturday morning he came over early to get Larry.

Usually David had better things to do than bother with Larry on a Saturday, so when he came, Larry didn't turn down the invitation to ride. He grabbed his battered blue helmet because he couldn't find his new one and hurried outside.

They rode directly to the Field. It was muddy, and none of the other boys were around.

"So take me to the house," David ordered with a satisfied grin. "There's nothing else to do."

That was what David had planned all along, Larry thought. Part of him wished he'd gone over to Stuart Olson's house to help work on Stuart's brother's car. He had told Stuart he'd probably come. But in another part of him a flame of excitement began to burn. He would never have been brave enough to go back to that house alone, and he did want to see it again.

"Okay," Larry said slowly. "We go to the house."

It took them a long time to ride at the side of the road as far as the big plowed field next to the house. When they got there, the field wasn't the same. Even rows of tiny green plants spread across it now, and water filled all the hollows.

At the far end they could see the long line of pine trees that marked the boundary of the house. Both boys shifted into low gear.

"Remember," Larry warned, "we don't go inside."

"Of course not," David agreed. But a glint of anticipation appeared in his brown eyes. "We just look around outside."

They rode past the last tree, and Larry quickly twisted his wheel to the right. He turned into the driveway, David following close behind.

They both stopped, unable to believe their eyes.

There was no house.

Larry blinked and looked again. The only building standing was the small shed at the end of the drive. Where the house had been was a pile of charred timber and twisted wires.

"Wow!" David said in an awed voice. "The whole thing's burned down. There's not a single wall left. Well, let's see what we can find." He parked his motorcycle behind the first pine, ready to make the best of the situation.

The needles of the large pine nearest the house had turned brown. Several of the lower branches had been broken off.

"Must have been some fire," Larry said. "I wish we'd known about it when it happened."

David's eyes sparkled. "Yeah, wouldn't that have

been something? They probably had a bunch of fire trucks."

He trotted over to where the house had been. Each of his footprints showed plainly in the muddy expanse that had once been a small lawn.

The boys took their time poking around at the edges of the foundation. Everything had fallen in a tangle into what had been the basement. Nothing looked like what it had been except a bathtub, which was half-full of rain water.

The stove and the table Larry had seen in the kitchen the week before had vanished. He could find nothing that resembled either one. Maybe the fire had started in the kitchen. Maybe one of the burners hadn't been quite turned off. But he remembered having looked at them closely. He was certain they'd been turned off.

"I'd like to jump down in there and get a few things," David said. He was looking with desire at some pieces of yellow tile near the bathtub.

Larry thought of the piece of hundred-dollar bill and the blue airline bag with its clippings. Those were what he'd like to find. But if even the furniture had burned, the bag would certainly be nothing but ashes.

He wished he'd read more of the clippings. He

wished he knew a lot more about what had been going on at the house.

He watched David hunch over, trying to find a way to climb down into the basement.

"Hey, you boys!" came an unexpected cry. "What are you doing here?"

3. Questions

Startled by the voice, both boys whirled.

A battered green-and-white pickup truck was in the driveway. Larry and David had been so interested in the burned house that they hadn't even heard the truck pull in. A round bald head with fringes of brown hair poked from the high window on the driver's side.

"It isn't a good idea to play here, boys. A place like this could be dangerous."

"What does he know?" David muttered.

Larry stared at the big bald man and the truck. It wasn't like him to begin a conversation, especially not with a stranger. But he'd never been so curious. He had to know.

"When did the house burn?" he asked, walking toward the pickup.

The man drew his head back inside and settled

himself comfortably. In that position he looked more friendly than he'd seemed at first. He even smiled at Larry, crinkling his eyes so the blue part hardly showed.

Larry smiled back, although he didn't feel friendly.

"Interested, eh?" the man said. "Well, I guess boys like to know what's happening. I didn't mean to scare you. Just wanted to warn you."

Behind him came the quick, low murmur of another voice. For the first time, Larry noticed the woman sitting on the passenger side. She was small, and her dark hair was streaked with blonde. She looked like one of the high school girls who'd tried to bleach her hair but never quite got it right.

While the man talked to her over his shoulder, Larry read the name printed on the side of the truck: E. Pilcher.

Mr. Pilcher turned back to him. "I've been out of town, but Bonnie says the fire was a week ago." He gazed past Larry toward the house. "First time I've seen it myself."

"What happened to the people who lived here?" Larry asked.

"Oh, the house was empty." Mr. Pilcher laughed.

"Been empty two or three years now, ever since old man Hartley died. He left it to his son and daughter. While they argued about whether or not to sell, the place just sat here."

"Wasn't one of them living in the house?" Larry asked. He felt confused. How could the house have been empty? He *knew* someone had been living there.

"One moved to Florida and one's in Maine," the bald man said. "They never could agree. They couldn't even agree to rent to someone who'd look after things."

Larry's throat felt so dry that he croaked when he talked. "Are you sure the house was empty?"

Mr. Pilcher turned to the woman again. She spoke softly, and Larry couldn't hear a word.

"I told you, nobody's lived here for years," the man repeated. "Not since Hartley died."

Mr. Pilcher stared at the ruins for a moment before he reached for the gear shift. "Well, we'll be moving on. You boys be careful, you hear?" The motor roared, and he backed out fast, splattering mud.

Larry and David looked at one another.

"He said nobody had lived here for years," Larry said slowly. "But that's not true. I know somebody was in that house."

"Probably the son or daughter came to stay for a

while, and Pilcher didn't know." David headed for his bike.

"Then why didn't they turn up when there was a fire?" Larry followed right on David's heels.

"Well," David said, "I guess it wasn't one of them. Unless there's a body down there somewhere." His eyes roamed over the ruins as if he wouldn't mind discovering a burned body.

"The firemen would have checked to be sure about that," Larry answered.

"Okay, how about this?" asked David, not at all discouraged. "The old man was having dinner with a friend. Just before they started to eat, Mr. Hartley got sick. The friend rushed him to the hospital. But the old man died, and nobody ever came back."

Larry shook his head. "Mr. Pilcher said Mr. Hartley died two or three years ago. That food had only been sitting around for a few days."

"Then it was a tramp, and he got scared away. Big deal. Who cares?" David began swinging his arms in bored circles. "This isn't any fun. I'm going back to find the guys."

"Now that things are getting good, you want to leave," Larry protested.

"I don't think anything's very good," David said.

"I wanted to poke around an empty house. Now that the house isn't here, there's nothing to do."

He started to mount his cycle, then paused as a car drove slowly past them, stopped, and backed up. It was a police car, and it turned into the driveway.

4. The Missing Helmet

Officer Foreman, the policeman who often patrolled their neighborhood, stepped from the car. Muscles rippled beneath his shirt. With his broad shoulders and strong legs, he looked like a man who spent hours lifting weights. Even though Foreman wasn't tall, any crook would think twice before tangling with such a tough guy.

"Morning, boys," the policeman said in a friendly way. "You're just the people I wanted to see. Aren't you part of the bunch that rides at Abbott's Field?"

They both hesitated before they nodded.

"Would you boys answer a few questions for me?"

"What kind of questions?" David demanded, instantly suspicious. He was always accused when something went wrong on their street. It sounded now as though Officer Foreman was going to accuse someone.

"Nothing too hard." Officer Foreman grinned. "Just wanted to hear what you know about this fire."

"We didn't even know there'd been a fire," David said. "When we saw the ruins, we stopped. And some guy in a truck was here a minute ago. He told us about the owner."

"I see. Ever been to this property before?"

Larry wondered if he should admit that he had. He certainly didn't want any trouble with the police. But David answered quickly, "First time. We just gave the bikes a tune-up, and we were out for a test run."

Officer Foreman nodded. "Pretty far for boys your age to ride."

"We're almost fourteen," David argued. "And it's not so far. We drove off the road, and we're not hurting anything here."

"I'm sure you're being careful." The policeman had stopped smiling. "What I wanted to ask was, do you know anybody who's been hanging around this house recently?"

Although he hated to admit he'd been inside the house, Larry thought his information might help the police. He opened his mouth to confess.

But again David answered first. "None of our guys have been here. Why? What difference does it make?"

"Well, we found a red helmet on the ground over there." Officer Foreman indicated a bush beside the drive. "We thought there might be a connection between that and the fire. We have a witness who saw a thin, dark-haired boy around here a few days ago. Could be he started the fire and left the helmet in his rush to get away."

Larry felt as if he'd been run over by a truck. His hand moved upward to the battered blue helmet on his head. That was why he couldn't find his red helmet! The beautiful new helmet was at the police station, and that wasn't the worst of it. Someone had seen him near the house. *He* was a thin, dark-haired boy. If he weren't wearing the old blue helmet, Officer Foreman could have seen that for himself.

"I'll ask around," David volunteered while Larry stood silent, too stunned to talk. "If one of the guys from our group left that helmet, I'll find out for you."

"Well, that's good of you." Officer Foreman was smiling again. "I'd appreciate that." He swung back into his police car and drove away.

"What's the matter with you?" David exploded when the policeman was gone. "You acted like you'd been caught lighting the match."

"I almost was," Larry groaned. "The Pilchers said

the fire was about a week ago. *I* was in the house a week ago today. Someone must have seen me. And I left my helmet. I forgot all about leaving it until just now. I thought it was at home somewhere."

"You've got your helmet on your head this very minute." David looked disgusted.

"This is my old helmet. You never saw the new one."

"Man! How could you be so dumb?"

"What should I do? Should I tell Officer Foreman I was in the house? I guess I have to." Head down, Larry started for his motorcycle.

David grabbed his arm with both hands. "Wait a minute. Never admit anything, don't you know that? Let him prove it was you."

"He can," Larry said. "He has my helmet."

"So?" David was frowning. "Was your name in it?"

"No."

"Then go buy another one."

"I can't. I don't have the money. Do you know how many times I had to babysit before I saved enough to buy the red one?"

"Well, you're out a helmet then. It's worth it to stay out of trouble. If my mom heard about this, she'd grab my bike and sell it so fast I'd be dizzy for a month. Come on, let's keep going in case Foreman stays on our tail. We can head back in a few minutes."

Larry was too upset to argue. He hadn't started any fire. He didn't know anything about it. But if he admitted the helmet was his, who'd believe he was innocent?

As he followed slowly behind David, he tried to control his panic. How could a little thing like a flat tire turn into such a big mess? Didn't he have enough trouble with his English? He couldn't even imagine the problems he'd have if his parents found out he was wanted by the police.

They passed a big white farmhouse with a white barn and a dark blue metal silo. No cars were in the drive, but a medium-sized bicycle without a seat was lying near the garage. A small brown dog jumped out from behind a tree and barked as long as he could see them. They rode faster to get away from him.

Around a bend they came to an old brick house. The green-and-white pickup truck they'd seen before was parked in that driveway. Larry and David paused to check out the truck and the house.

David picked at the braces on his front teeth with his thumb. "Well, now we've found out where that man Pilcher lives. In case you wanted to know, which I didn't."

"Do you think one of the Pilchers was the person who saw me?" Larry's voice trembled slightly. He could imagine the Pilchers saying they'd seen him at the house. Then Officer Foreman would show up to arrest him.

"The Pilchers aren't the ones. They would have said something when they were talking to us." David sounded very experienced. "Nobody knows you were there. Forget about it, and let's get back home."

They began to turn around but stopped when a small tan truck pulled up beside them. Inside the covered back were ladders, lumber, dozens of boxes, and a strange-looking cupboard.

"Say, boys," the driver called, "want to do me a favor?"

"What is it?" David—as usual—wanted to know before he agreed to anything.

"I just built Mrs. Pilcher a corner cabinet for her dining room. She lives in that brick house over there. How'd you fellows like to carry it over to their porch for me?"

"Why not?" was Larry's instant response. If the Pilchers were going to recognize him, better now than later. Let them have one more good look.

David stared at him as if he'd lost his mind.

Leaving the motor running, the carpenter climbed stiffly from his truck. He was a thin man with wispy white hair. He moved as if he was very tired and would like to sit still and rest for a long time.

"I'm Ames," he said. "You boys live along here?"

"In the Blue Meadows subdivision," Larry told him.

"That so?" asked Mr. Ames. "Well, I work over to that part of town sometimes. You're a long ways from home. I guess having those machines takes you a good distance pretty quick."

"Yeah, it does," Larry said.

Mr. Ames went around to the back of his truck. Opening the tailgate, he lifted out the tall corner cabinet. He let one end rest on the ground and leaned the other end in Larry's arms.

"Careful carrying this, son," the carpenter warned. "There's no sidewalk, and the yard's pretty muddy. I was here the other day to measure. Slipped and almost took a bad fall. That's why I don't care to tackle it again."

"Do you do a lot of work for the Pilchers?" Larry asked, sorry he'd offered to help.

"Happens I do. Ned and his wife are fixing up this old house better than new. They move around town, buying and fixing and selling. I helped with their last one, too."

Mr. Ames slammed the truck door and started back to the driver's seat.

"Did you know a house burned down near here?" Larry asked as Mr. Ames hoisted himself back to his seat.

The old man settled himself, blinking several times. "Oh, sure, I know about the fire. It was the Hartley house that burned. I knew Boyd Hartley years ago. He was a good farmer, a man who loved his land."

"Nobody was living there, right?" Larry wanted to be certain he had everything straight. That was very important to him.

"Nobody's been there since Boyd died." Mr. Ames's thoughts seemed to be far away, although he kept talking. "His children were friends of my girl years ago, you know. I always said those two didn't know a fine piece of property when they saw it. Left the place empty for so long, the house was finally burned down by vandals. Too bad. My friends the Pilchers were hoping to buy it. They had the key, and they looked inside more than once."

Startled, Larry leaned forward. "Do you think the house was burned on purpose?"

"No doubt about it," Mr. Ames announced. He jerked his sharp chin up and down. "Last Saturday night it was. The fire department boys found all the evidence to prove arson. My friends in the department said whoever did it left an empty can of gasoline. Of course, they'll never catch the person. They never do. With an empty house like that, there isn't much to go on."

The old man gave a disgusted grunt. "The world is changing. People who ought to know what's right don't act like they're supposed to anymore. Look what happened here."

Without warning, Mr. Ames started his truck moving. In a moment he was gone.

"All *right*," said David, whose silence until then had been very unlike him. "The house was torched! And it happened just a few hours after you were there."

The muscles in Larry's arms and legs felt so rubbery that he could hardly support the heavy cabinet. "I knew something strange was going on at that house."

"You didn't know anything," David scoffed. "So the house was burned on purpose. That doesn't mean the fire had anything to do with what you saw inside."

"It could have," Larry insisted.

"You know all about engines," David said nastily. "You don't know much else."

Larry's certainty drained away. David was right about him. He *didn't* know much. How could he prove anything, even that he hadn't started the fire? His brain felt overloaded, and his arms ached. He needed time to think.

"Help me get this up to the house."

"I'm not going to go slipping around in the mud just because you wanted to do a good deed." David finished turning his motorcycle back the way they'd come.

"I can't carry this alone. Besides, your shoes are messed up already from walking around the burned house." That corner cabinet was going to tear his arms off if he couldn't let go of it soon. Larry didn't know how Mr. Ames had lifted it down from the truck all by himself.

"Okay," David agreed finally. His eyes flickered the way they did when he had a scheme. "But you promise not to talk to anyone about the Hartley house. And stop asking questions about it. The whole gang could get in trouble if people start thinking we're setting fires."

He was right, of course. Larry hadn't thought about the guys. Why couldn't he think as fast as David did? They both had to keep their mouths shut. It was better to lose his helmet and avoid trouble, that was for sure. If he kept what he knew a secret, nothing would happen to any of them.

5. *Keeping the Secret*

"Let's ring the bell and run," David suggested when they reached the long wooden porch.

They didn't have a chance to run or even to ring the bell. The door opened before they reached it, and big, bald Mr. Pilcher stood looking down at them. He was even larger standing up than he'd seemed sitting in his truck.

"What are you two doing here?" he demanded, although it should have been obvious.

Neither boy said anything as they lowered the cabinet onto the porch. Larry was afraid Mr. Pilcher would recognize him, and he knew David was annoyed because he hadn't wanted to help. Finally Larry decided it was better to say something than stand waiting to be accused.

"Uh, Mr. Ames asked us to bring this cabinet to your wife. He was scared he'd slip and fall if he tried to carry it. He said—uh—your yard's muddy."

Mr. Pilcher roared with laughter. Wondering what he'd said that was funny, Larry waited uneasily.

"No mud in the driveway," Mr. Pilcher sputtered, "just a little in the yard. That Ames! His mind is playing tricks. Ever since his daughter's family packed up and moved out of state, he's been different. Guess he misses her and those two boys."

Mr. Pilcher had stopped laughing. He was staring at the motorcycles and looking very serious. Did he recognize one? Larry clenched his hands together behind his back.

But all Mr. Pilcher said was, "I've seen boys on bikes like yours at Abbott's Field. You must be part of that group. And now you're all the way out here. Well, I'd have done the same at your age. You must get all over town. I'll bet you know plenty about what goes on in these parts."

Larry hunched his shoulders and shot a worried glance at David. David was smart—it was better if he handled things.

"You mean, do we know anything about how the fire started?" David asked the question right out.

"I didn't mean that exactly. But if you did see something, Mr. Hartley's son or daughter might want to offer a reward for information," Mr. Pilcher said. His voice had turned as smooth as honey.

There was no accusation. Pilcher might suspect him, but the man wasn't sure. Larry was so relieved that he almost melted into a little heap right there on the porch. But he knew he had to keep thinking. He tried a comment of his own. "I guess the son and daughter were the ones who left the electricity on and the phone hooked up."

Mr. Pilcher snorted. "Nobody was living there. The electricity was left on so the furnace would work and the pipes wouldn't freeze during the winter. The phone was taken out. Too expensive to have a phone in an empty house. What makes you think those utilities were connected?"

There was no answer Larry could give. How could he have been stupid enough to mention the phone and the electricity?

As if he were seeing the boys for the first time, Mr. Pilcher suddenly grinned. "Come on inside. Have a Coke. We'll talk some. I think my wife has cookies, too."

"My mother expects us for lunch," David said. He sounded grown-up and polite, for a change.

"Thanks, anyway," Larry added, again grateful for David's quick thinking.

"My wife likes boys," Mr. Pilcher said insistently. "We'd like to hear what you two do to keep busy. And we might have some suggestions."

"Maybe another time." Larry shoved David, and they moved quickly off the porch and through the yard. Larry took a peek back over his shoulder. The tall bald man was standing in his doorway with his arms folded over his chest. He hadn't touched the cabinet.

At the window that overlooked the porch, the curtains were moving. Someone must be standing there, waiting for them to leave. Or did he have it wrong? Maybe someone had been waiting for them to come *in*.

Larry shivered and walked even faster. He reached the motorcycles before David.

"How come you're in such a hurry?" David asked.

"I didn't like that guy asking us inside. He wanted something. You couldn't have paid me to go inside their house."

David grinned. "Maybe he would have held us for ransom. Maybe if we'd gone in there, we'd never have come out again."

David must have scared himself because he didn't waste any time jumping on his bike. They both roared away as fast as they could.

Larry didn't feel comfortable again until he was at David's house eating lunch. Mrs. Wallace gave them juicy hamburgers inside buns with seeds on top. David picked off as many seeds as he could, but Larry liked the seeds. He even ate the ones left on his plate after the hamburger was gone.

As soon as he felt less hungry, Larry's thoughts bounced back to the Hartley house. "I still don't understand," he complained between bites of his second hamburger.

David set down his milk. "Understand what?"

"Mr. Ames said the house was empty." Larry had to stop to swallow. "So did Mr. Pilcher. Only I know it wasn't empty. I know someone was staying there."

"No, you don't." David flicked a seed across the table at Larry. "You don't know that. All you know is that some tramp went in and turned on the lights and started to cook. And then he left."

"The important thing is, nobody else knows that," Larry stated. He added a generous amount of catsup to his third hamburger. "Mr. Ames said he had friends in the fire department. And they thought the house was empty."

David wiped at the white line of milk on his upper lip. "Remember whatever you know is a secret. We won't even say anything to the other guys for a while. There's no sense all of us being in trouble because you were dumb and left your helmet. Forget you were ever there!"

"Okay, okay." Larry licked his lips, thinking how everything had gone wrong. At first he'd enjoyed impressing David with the story about exploring the empty house, but Larry hadn't counted on the house burning down. He'd never thought he could be identified as the boy who'd been there. How could he have been such a dope as to forget his helmet? And then his stupid questions probably made things worse. None of this would have happened to someone like David.

6. Someone Is Watching

"Let's get over to the Field," David said. "The rest of the guys should be around by now. Maybe Jimmy Rollins got his new motorcycle."

"Hey, that's right." Larry was glad to avoid any argument. He needed time to think.

"I sure would like to get my hands on a brand new motorcycle," David said.

"Only, you know those clerks when you go in a store," Larry said. "They never let you get the feel of handling one of those big bikes."

David grinned. "All they have to do is see me coming. Everything gets covered up or locked up. My dad doesn't want me near the big bikes, either. That's why I got a used cycle. And the smallest one they make."

"That's why the rest of us got the same thing." Larry smiled back. "Let's go see if Jimmy's any luckier."

Halfway out the front door, they were stopped by Mrs. Wallace. "David? Where are you going?"

Mrs. Wallace always looked to Larry as if she'd

been washed too many times. She had a pale, freckled face, light brown eyes, and faded red hair. She was always worried about terrible things that might happen to David. Some of them did happen because David was quick and reckless and never thought before he did whatever he wanted.

"We're going riding at the Field," David told her.

His mother nodded, looking more worried than before. "Sometimes I wish spring hadn't come. You're going to be out on that motorcycle morning, noon, and night. I just can't keep up with you. Something terrible is going to happen because of that motorcycle, I just know it. At least you're with Larry. He'll stay out of trouble. He's a good, sensible boy."

"Sure, Mom," David agreed. As soon as they were outside, he made his voice whiny like his mother's. "At least you're a good, sensible boy, Larry."

Embarrassed, Larry punched David's arm, looking as fierce as he could. "I stay out of trouble," he growled.

David laughed. "If she only knew," he said. "But you'd better make sure she never does."

"I said I wouldn't tell," Larry muttered. He didn't feel happy about making the promise, but he didn't know what else he could do. He couldn't take the chance of losing the friendship of David and the other bikers.

They headed for the Field. At the corner, Larry and David passed a parked police car. Just the sight of it made Larry's neck prickle although he knew Officer Foreman often lingered in that spot. They thought he liked to watch their workouts. Larry and David waved, and the policeman raised a casual hand. He was talking to one of the bikers.

Was Officer Foreman questioning each boy as he passed? He must remember them from that morning because he didn't stop them. Larry took a deep breath and hurried after David. As long as he kept quiet, he was safe from being arrested.

At the edge of the Field, everyone was gathered around a skinny boy wearing a shiny gold helmet. Between his legs he balanced a bright gold motorcycle.

"It's bigger than ours!" David shouted.

They rushed over to join the other boys.

Since Jimmy Rollins was generous, everyone who owned a bike was allowed a ride on his new one. They only used the short strip of paved road because the Field was too muddy for the shiny new bike.

In line to take his turn, Larry listened to Jimmy talking to Bob Macey. "Did Officer Foreman stop you on the way in? About a fire out in the country?"

Bob nodded. "Glad I didn't know anything about it. Somebody's going to have a big problem when Foreman catches up with him."

Larry chanced a quick glance over to the spot where Officer Foreman had been parked. The police car was gone. But to his surprise, a truck was in its place.

Larry stared at the green-and-white pickup truck. He was too far away to be sure, but the truck looked like the battered one Mr. Pilcher owned. Why would Mr. Pilcher come to watch them ride?

He turned to ask David, but David had got tired of waiting. He was on his motorcycle, zooming across the middle of the Field. An arching spray of muddy water filled the air behind him.

Another boy tried the same thing. Soon everyone was zipping madly back and forth, spraying and being sprayed. Before the afternoon was over, they were all soaking wet and covered with mud. Larry forgot about everything else.

"What have you been doing?" his mother demanded when he came home.

Her tone was sharp because she wanted things to be neat and pretty, just like she was. Larry knew he didn't look at all neat. He didn't do much explaining but just let her shoo him toward the shower.

After he found dry clothing, Larry clattered into the family room where his little sister, Linda, was watching television. It was a program about seals. Linda loved animals, and she wouldn't turn around to talk, even when Larry poked her.

Soon the program broke off, and an ad for fire insurance came on. When Larry watched the announcer in the fire hat, he thought about the Hartley house again. He had a strong feeling he wouldn't be out of trouble until the police found the person who'd set that fire. Who had been at the house? And why were they there? How could he find out more?

Sitting up straight, he called, "Mom, where's the newspaper?"

There was no answer.

He remembered he was supposed to go where his mother was instead of bellowing through the house like a wounded moose. When he reached the kitchen, Mrs. Kenniston was standing by the refrigerator waiting for him.

"I can't find the Meadowvale paper."

"On the coffee table in the family room. Or outside in the garage ready to be bundled for the paper drive."

Mrs. Kenniston smiled. "I'm not used to saving reading material for you."

Larry wished he hadn't asked. Most of the time his mother didn't seem to notice that he never read. He liked it that way. Then there was less chance she'd think to ask how he was doing in English.

"I'll probably do more reading when I'm older." He grinned cheerfully, hoping what he said would be true.

His mother sighed. "I just don't understand why you never read. Do your eyes bother you?"

"Not really." Larry started to edge away.

He located the paper he wanted and turned the pages slowly, reading each headline. It took a long time to find the small item he was searching for.

FARMHOUSE BURNS. Late Saturday night the empty Hartley farmhouse burned to the ground. Fire department investigators blame the conflagration on vandals, who used gasoline to set the blaze. The property has been abandoned since the death of Boyd Hartley, a prominent farmer in this community for over forty years. Present owners of the property have been notified but had no comment on the fire.

That was all there was. Disappointed, Larry read

the article again. He'd expected more information. He knew the police were investigating, but the article didn't mention them. Was there other evidence besides the helmet? If the police had any, the paper didn't say.

He wished Officer Foreman had seen the plates on the table and the glass of milk and the mug for coffee. A policeman would have known if they were important. The milk could have been for a kid, Larry thought. And the coffee? A grownup must have been there, too. David said a tramp had started to cook a meal and then been scared away. It would have had to be two tramps, Larry decided.

If only he'd taken a better look at those clothes. Who would have left a shirt and pants? And why? Maybe the person had had to take them off because they were wet or dirty. He might have borrowed something left by old man Hartley. Larry made a face, grateful he could come home to change when he wanted to. He wouldn't have liked to wear the clothes of someone he didn't even know.

Maybe the person who'd changed clothes hadn't had any choice. A picture of a man and boy flashed into his mind—a kidnapper and his victim. The Hartley house would have been a perfect place for a kidnapper to hide. Nobody would have noticed if two people stayed there for a few days. And after the ransom was paid, they would have left.

Larry remembered the story David had told him about a kidnapped boy. After the ransom was paid, the boy was found safe. Suddenly, Larry wondered if a million dollars in hundred-dollar bills would fit into an airline bag like the one he'd seen in the house.

7. Kidnappers!

"You're crazy!" David exploded when Larry explained his theory about a kidnapping. They were in gym class on Monday morning. "Go back to fixing motorcycles and stay out of this. Whatever happened, we don't want anything to do with it. How many times do I have to tell you?"

"I thought we should go to the library to find out more about the kidnapping you mentioned. It might be too important to leave alone." Larry tried not to shout back. The more quiet he was, the less likely he was to be noticed by the P.E. teacher. He didn't need any more problems with teachers.

"The library?" David's face turned as red as his hair. "No way."

"You have to help read the newspapers. That's where the story will be. Come on, Dave." Larry hated himself for begging. He wouldn't have had to if he could read the papers himself, but he could never read that much in one sitting. "It won't take long."

"I've got a football meeting this afternoon over at the high school. I've got to be ready to make the team in the fall. If it's so important to you, you figure out how to do that reading yourself." David brushed past him to line up for baseball.

The first ones in line got to pitch and catch. Most of the others ended up in the outfield. Usually Larry would have rushed to get in line because he liked to catch. This time he only glared after David and trotted straight out to the far corner of the field.

His idea had seemed like such a good one. If the local paper had news about the fire, the Chicago paper would have news about the kidnapping. He wanted to know who was kidnapped, and exactly which days he was missing. Then Larry would know if the boy could have been held at the Hartley house. Why couldn't David understand that they had to find out if the Hartley house was used in the kidnapping?

"Hey, Larry, what're you thinking about?"

He hadn't even noticed Stuart Olson come to stand beside him. Stuart was a new boy in school. He had a square, cheerful face, but somehow he hadn't made many friends yet.

"Thought you were coming over Saturday," Stuart said. "I called, but your mother said you'd gone off with David Wallace."

"We were checking out the bikes," Larry said.

"Oh." Stuart bent his shaggy blond head and looked at his feet as if he'd never noticed them before.

"Look, maybe your mom will let you get one," Larry added. "Then you could ride with us."

"It's not my mom who hates motorcycles—it's my dad," Stuart told him, still looking down. "One of his best friends was killed in a bike accident. Dad just doesn't think they're safe."

"I'd never ride one in the street. Or without a helmet. That's what's dangerous." Larry kept one eye on the first batter, who was settling into his stance.

The pitch sailed over the plate, the bat cracked, and a high fly shot toward them. While Larry wondered if he should make a try, somebody else rushed past and grabbed it. Stuart seemed surprised the game had started.

"We only ride the trails," Larry continued. "That's very safe."

"My dad's friend was out in a field," Stuart answered. "Then he ran into a tree."

There wasn't much answer for that. But Larry

knew he was too good a rider to ever crash into a tree. And he still thought it was a shame Stuart couldn't ride just because some old guy was careless. Stuart seemed like a nice kid.

"Hey, you doing anything after school?" Larry asked suddenly. He'd just remembered what a good student Stuart was. That probably meant he was a good reader, too.

Another ball zoomed straight at them. Stuart took a step back to make an easy catch, but the ball slipped through his hands and bounced away. While Stuart searched helplessly, another player grabbed the ball.

"Pay attention!" roared David from the infield. "Where'd you learn to play ball, anyway? At the zoo?"

Several boys laughed. The gym teacher blew his whistle in short, angry blasts. Stuart's face turned white, and he moved away. He crouched awkwardly, concentrating on the next pitch.

"Meet me in front," Larry said, but he wasn't sure Stuart was listening.

After school he stood beside the main door, watching for Stuart. David and three other football players went by, and David didn't even say hello. What a jerk, Larry thought. Those guys thought they were wonderful, but David didn't even recognize real excitement when it came along. He'd show David he could do something besides fix motorcycles. He'd prove he was right about kidnappers at the Hartley house.

As Larry waited, he became more and more angry. David wouldn't help, and Stuart wasn't coming, either. He couldn't do that reading alone. Okay, he'd go home. He'd never find out about the house, and he'd never see his helmet again. Nobody else cared, so why should he?

He stomped along the sidewalk, kicking at a stone.

"Hey, Larry! You still want me?"

In the time it took Larry to turn around, his scowl became a smile. "Sure do!" he shouted. "Come with me to the library."

The eagerness on Stuart's face faded. "Library?"

"Yeah. Promise you won't tell anybody, and I'll let you in on something."

"Okay." Stuart brushed a hand backward through his shaggy hair. If he didn't do that all the time, Larry thought, his hair wouldn't look so much like a lawn that needed mowing.

As they walked, Larry told Stuart he thought someone in Meadowvale was a kidnapper. He described the house where he thought the kidnapper had hidden out.

"Kidnappers are creeps." Stuart ruffled his hair back and forth until it was a tangle of straw. "I hope we can help catch them."

By the time they reached the library, they were ready to capture all the kidnappers in the Chicago area.

"Ask the librarian for what you want," Stuart whispered as they stepped inside.

"Sure," Larry agreed, as if he'd known all along. He didn't tell Stuart he'd never been inside the public library before. His mother brought his little sister once a week for picture books, but Larry would never come with them. He only used the school library when he had to.

He looked curiously at the large room. On the right side were floor-to-ceiling racks of books. Small tables and chairs and low bookcases were arranged on the left side. In the center was a long counter.

The woman behind the counter smiled at them. She looked a lot like Larry's kindergarten teacher. He hoped the librarian liked kids as well as that teacher had.

Before he could speak, Larry had to swallow and clear his throat. "I'd, uh, like newspapers," he croaked.

"We subscribe to several papers. Which one did you wish?" The librarian smiled again, and he decided she did like kids. Words came more easily then.

He explained that they wanted the Chicago papers for the past three weeks. The librarian didn't seem to find anything strange about that. She took Larry and Stuart past the children's section into the Reference Room. After they sat down at a long table, she brought an armload of papers and arranged them in front of the boys.

"Look for anything you can find about kidnapping," Larry told Stuart. He shoved the pile toward him.

Stuart took the top paper and started reading headlines. His eyes scanned the page four times as fast as Larry's did. Reading was going to hurt, Larry thought, staring at the small print. But he had to do it.

He stumbled from headline to headline. One told about counterfeit money being passed, and several mentioned robberies. By the time he'd finished one section of one paper, Stuart had finished an entire newspaper and started another.

Forehead crinkled, Larry kept reading. A young man had escaped from the state prison farm, which was about fifty miles from Meadowvale. The guys always joked about how they'd be alert to spot an escaped prisoner if one ever got away. Then, when one did escape, they never even heard about it. Wait until he told David they'd missed their chance for a motorcycle search—if he ever told David anything again.

Stuart was going through his fourth paper—and Larry was still on his first—when Stuart asked, "What's this?" He shoved a page at Larry, pointing to a column with one finger.

The words *Boy Missing* stood out in big, black letters. If he hadn't known you had to be quiet in a library, Larry would have asked Stuart to read it to him.

The long words were confusing, but he struggled with them silently. The boy who was missing turned out to live in a suburb about six miles north of Meadowvale. That made sense, Larry decided. Hiding the boy at the Hartley house was like keeping him in his own backyard.

"I think this is the one," he told Stuart. "Keep reading. See if there's any more about that boy."

He sat back in his chair to rest his eyes and sniffed at the unfamiliar smell of the library. It was a nice bookish smell. A shaft of late afternoon sun lingered on a rack of magazines. They looked bright and inviting.

Larry sighed and began to study the photograph beside the kidnapping article. Michael Courtney was the boy's name. Michael had a round face and dark hair. Officer Foreman said a witness had seen a dark-haired boy near the Hartley house. Maybe the witness had seen Michael.

Encouraged, Larry checked more headlines, but no other stories about the missing boy turned up. Stuart didn't find anything else, either. Then, in the Wednesday paper of two weeks before, Larry found another article.

> The twelve-year-old son of a suburban businessman was kidnapped on his way to school last Friday and held until Tuesday evening. Before the boy was released, his father paid a hundred-thousand-dollar ransom.

Deciphering the long paragraphs that followed was as hard for Larry as weeding the whole front lawn. His shirt was damp by the time he came to the end.

> Michael Courtney was released unharmed after a ransom drop in the Civic Building. J. M. Johnson, Assistant FBI Director in charge of the local office, said two men are being sought in the kidnapping.

Larry wriggled his stiff shoulders and took a deep

breath. His eyes ached from straining to read, but the pain was worth it.

"Here, check this," he whispered.

Stuart took the article and read it in three seconds. "You think he's the one?" he asked, passing it back.

"I'm going to copy it," Larry said. "Will you keep reading?"

Stuart nodded and reached for another newspaper. Larry took out his school notebook and started scrib-

bling. Writing took him a long time, too, but it was easier than reading.

By the time he was finished, Stuart had skimmed through the rest of the papers.

"Did you find what you wanted?" the librarian asked when they gave back the newspapers. She sounded as if it mattered.

"Yes, thanks." Larry tried to arrange the stack neatly.

"You're quite welcome. Come back any time," she said, smiling her nice smile.

Larry took one last look at the tall stacks of books. There must be thousands of things in them that he'd like to know. He felt a little sorry he wouldn't be back. But he wasn't meant to be a reader. It was too bad, but there was no changing that kind of thing.

In the corridor, a tall, rangy man standing with an open book in his hand caught Larry's eye. What was Mr. Pilcher doing at the library? Funny how everywhere he went lately, Mr. Pilcher was there, too. No, it wasn't funny—it was scary. Was he watching because he thought Larry had set one fire and might start another? Was he the witness who had seen Larry at the house?

He grabbed Stuart's arm. "Let's get out of here."

As soon as they were outside, Stuart asked, "What's the big rush? And how do you know we found the right article?"

Larry spoke with confidence. "The days Michael was missing were the week before the fire. Two people were involved, and that fits with what I saw. I think one man made calls and arranged the ransom. The other stayed with the kidnapped boy. When the partner in Chicago called Tuesday evening to say he had the money, the other kidnapper and the boy rushed out of the house without eating their supper."

"What fire?" Stuart asked.

"Uh-oh." Larry jammed his hand over his mouth. He was about as dumb as David said he was. "I can't tell you about that yet. But I will as soon as I can."

Stuart ducked his head to hide his hurt expression. Embarrassed, Larry turned back toward the library. Mr. Pilcher had come outside and stood on the steps watching them. Larry felt certain now he was being followed.

Suddenly, a weird idea came to him. Mr. Pilcher knew the Hartley house was empty because he lived close by. He even had a key. He was supposed to have been out of town during the days of the kidnapping. Maybe, instead, *he* was at the Hartley house, keeping

Michael prisoner. Maybe he saw Larry at the house, afterward. If he had, he'd want to know how much Larry knew. That would explain why he invited Larry and David inside his house just to talk, and why he went to the Field later to see what they were doing. It would even explain why he was in the library. He must have been worried about what they were going to do after school, and so he'd followed Larry to find out.

"Stuart," Larry said, "I think I know who the kidnapper is."

"You do?" Stuart sounded very impressed. "How could you tell that from the newspaper?"

"Things just started to add up. I saw something that started me thinking."

"What?"

Larry shook his head. "It may turn out I'm wrong, so I don't want to say anything."

Only he didn't think he was wrong. Mr. Pilcher wouldn't be watching him without a good reason. But even if he went to the police and told them everything he knew, would they believe his story?

8. A Risky Plan

After he and Stuart said goodbye, Larry raced the last two blocks home. It was later than he'd thought. He dashed inside and found his father already sitting at the kitchen table waiting for supper.

"Where have you been, son?" Mr. Kenniston looked up from his newspaper.

"I had some work to do at the library."

Although Mr. Kenniston didn't comment, he nodded with satisfaction, as if he thought Larry were shaping up at last. With his father so pleased, here was a good chance to tell about everything he'd found out. Things were getting out of control, and he wanted a grown-up to know what had happened.

But how could he begin? If he told about the house, he'd have to say how he'd found it. His mother was still too angry about nearly missing the wedding for him to risk that.

He couldn't confess until he had proof that kidnappers had used the Hartley house. Then nobody could be angry with him.

As Larry hesitated, his mother turned around from the stove. "Before I forget," she said, "I want to tell you I made an appointment to have your eyes checked. It's for Friday after school."

"Why did you do that?" Larry wasn't pleased at all. His eyes were checked every year at school, and he'd never got a slip saying he needed further examination. Lots of people did get slips.

"Just thought it might be a good idea," was all his mother answered. "Your grades aren't as good as they should be. Maybe we've overlooked some problem, and I thought it might be your vision."

Larry hung up his windbreaker and hurried to throw his books on his bed. After a few seconds, he slid into his chair at the table. His favorite dinner was waiting: roast beef, hot cornbread, and peas. Everyone else was ready to begin. They were practically holding their forks over their plates as they waited for him.

Once again Larry wished he could tell his mother and father about the Hartley house. David liked keeping his parents in the dark about what he was doing, but Larry felt guilty when he did. Even though he bragged to David about hiding his failing report in English, he felt bad about fooling his parents. He'd almost convinced himself that he should tell about the house when his sister started talking.

"I saw the new neighbor today," Linda announced. "On my way home from kindergarten."

"She means Mrs. Barnwell, I think," said Mrs. Kenniston to her husband. "Remember? They moved in last week. They're going to come here some evening to visit after they get settled."

"I talked to Mrs. Barnwell," Linda said. "But she's not who I mean. I mean Rani."

"I didn't know they had children," said Mr. Kenniston. "Is Ronnie your age?"

"They *don't* have children," Mrs. Kenniston said.

Both parents looked at Linda. "Who's Ronnie?"

"Rani is their cat. That's an Indian name, Mrs. Barnwell said. It means 'queen.' Rani's black and white and awful thin. They can't find anything she'll eat."

"How about cat food?" Larry suggested, becoming interested in spite of his own problems.

"She *hates* cat food," Linda informed him.

"Why won't she eat cat food?" Mr. Kenniston asked, sounding puzzled.

"All she likes is water-buffalo meat." Linda nodded her small head emphatically.

"Water-buffalo meat?" Larry exploded into loud laughter. "Where would anyone buy water-buffalo meat?"

Linda's triumph was destroyed. Her small face puckered into a frown that was near tears.

Her mother rescued her. "She's right. I heard about that, but I forgot. The Barnwells were living in India. The cat was fed water-buffalo meat, which was very cheap to buy there. Naturally, there's nothing like it here, and they can't find anything the cat likes instead. When I talked to her, Mrs. Barnwell was very worried. I'm sorry to hear the cat still isn't eating."

"I remember a cat that wouldn't eat," said Mr. Kenniston. "When I was a boy, a neighbor lady fed her cat nothing but salmon. Then she couldn't buy any salmon for some reason. The cat wouldn't eat anything else. I think it starved to death."

Linda stared at him with horror. "Will that happen to Rani?" A big tear trembled at the corner of one eye. "Poor Rani."

Mr. Kenniston realized he'd made a mistake and

tried to retreat. "That won't happen to Rani, honey. That was a long time ago. Cats were probably different."

"I think," said Mrs. Kenniston firmly, "that this cat will start eating soon. Don't worry, Linda. It will get used to our food and be fine."

"Can I take Rani some roast beef and cornbread?" Linda wanted to know. "Maybe that would taste like water buffalo to her."

"We'll see," was all Mrs. Kenniston would say.

Larry knew that meant "no," but Linda looked hopeful. She hadn't learned yet that "we'll see" at their house meant "forget it."

At the bus stop Tuesday morning, Larry told about the cat that would eat only water-buffalo meat. David, especially, thought the story was very funny. He repeated it to other people as they arrived. Everyone began making suggestions about foods to try. Most of the suggestions weren't very practical, but David took a pencil out of his pocket and pretended to write them all down in his social studies book.

Warmed by the uproar, Larry felt more friendly toward David. He decided he'd try to talk to him once more about the house, the kidnappers, and Mr. Pilcher. David was in just as good a mood, and they arranged to meet after school.

When Larry got to David's house that afternoon, his friend was washing his motorcycle. The hose sent a stream of water rushing down the drive. David, with bare feet, stood happily in the middle of his river.

"It's as hot as summer," David greeted him cheerfully.

"You don't expect weather like this before June," Larry agreed. Too impatient to waste any time, he held out the sheet of notebook paper on which he'd copied the newspaper article about the kidnapping.

"What's this?" David took it in a wet hand and glanced without interest at the sprawling handwriting.

"Read it," Larry said.

"Nobody could read that ant trail. Just tell me what it says."

"It's the best I can write. And don't get it wet." Larry grabbed at the paper. "Give it back. I'll read it to you."

David wiped his hands on his jeans and took the paper again. The threat of Larry trying to read aloud was enough to make him read the copied article himself.

"Hey," David said when he finally understood. "This must be the kid my father was talking about last week. Where'd you find it?"

"At the library. In the Chicago paper. Stuart and I read papers for the last three weeks."

"I didn't know you were that interested. I could have asked my dad more about it." David handed back the wet, limp paper.

"You knew I was interested. I told you yesterday in school." Larry folded the paper and put it into his shirt pocket.

Why did David have to be like that? Larry was tempted to go home, but who else would help him find out about the house? He couldn't return there alone, and Stuart had no bike.

"I had to think football yesterday," David excused himself. "Now I can think about this."

"And I told you *why* I was interested," Larry said, fighting to be patient. "I think we found the place where they kept that boy while they were waiting for the ransom to be paid."

To Larry's great satisfaction, David's brown eyes began to sparkle with enthusiasm. So Larry described how the information in the kidnapping articles explained the uneaten food he'd seen at the house. He told about seeing Mr. Pilcher at the library and his new suspicion that Pilcher was the kidnapper.

While listening, David turned off the hose and

polished his motorcycle with an old shirt. Soon he was listening more than polishing.

"Now we have to go back to that house to see if any evidence is left," Larry finished. Going back was the most important part. Had he persuaded David they *had* to go?

"Go back out there? Why?" David snapped his cloth, sounding unpersuaded.

"Michael Courtney, the kidnapped boy, might have left something," Larry explained. "If we found it, we could give it to the police. They'd solve the kidnapping, and we wouldn't be in any trouble. I might even get my helmet back."

"And the other bikers would really be jealous if we turned out to be heroes." David laughed, but then he shook his head. "You figured everything out all right. I've got to hand it to you. But you forgot one thing."

"What?" Larry demanded.

"You forgot about whoever set the fire." David sat down on the porch step and reached for his shoes and socks. "What if Pilcher *is* the kidnapper and burned the house because he saw you there the first Saturday? If he sees you hanging around any more, he could get *real* nervous. You don't know what he might do."

Larry took a deep breath and sat beside David on the step. He didn't like to think about Mr. Pilcher being dangerous, although the idea had been lurking in the back of his mind.

"If it is Pilcher, he's had plenty of time to get rid of any evidence," David warned. "If you don't show up any more, he'll forget about you. You'll be safe, and so will the rest of us. My mother would collapse if she thought I was mixed up in something like this."

"I'm sure there's some kind of evidence left," Larry insisted. "I know I can find it if I have a chance."

David snorted his disagreement as he finished tying his shoe. "Okay, I'll go with you once more right now. Only if we don't find anything, you forget the whole thing, promise?"

Larry agreed quickly. He never knew which way David would jump. Just when he was certain David would make some excuse not to go, he went along.

Well, this was great! Larry was positive that once they got to the house, they'd find proof that the kidnappers had been there. He didn't know what the evidence could be, but he knew he'd recognize it when he saw it.

9. The Clue in the Shed

For the third time in ten days, Larry approached the tall pines marking the drive of the Hartley house. He and David roared around the corner, stopping short when they found a small tan truck parked in the shadows.

"What's Mr. Ames doing here?" Larry asked.

David shrugged and drew up on the driver's side of the truck. Larry followed.

"Afternoon." The old man peered out of his open window and dropped a piece of orange peel. He slipped a section of orange into his mouth.

"Heard anything more about the fire?" David asked.

Larry was almost afraid to hear the answer. What if the police were after him? The clerk at the store where he bought his helmet might have given them a description. Luckily, he'd paid the cash he'd saved from babysitting. The store wouldn't have his name.

"Nothing new." Mr. Ames wiped juice from his sharp chin.

"If your friends the firemen knew something, they'd tell you, wouldn't they?" Larry tried to sound casual.

"Happens they would. But they haven't." Mr. Ames's blue eyes seemed keener than Larry had noticed before. "Do *you* know anything?"

"Who, me?" Larry could feel his heart speed up. "If I did, I'd go straight to the police." It wasn't exactly a lie. When he had his evidence, he *would* go to Officer Foreman.

Holding an orange section halfway to his mouth, Mr. Ames studied him. "That's exactly what you should do."

Larry was afraid he'd said too much. What if Mr. Ames warned Mr. Pilcher? They must be friends. They worked together fixing up houses. He decided he should change the subject.

"Do you come here very often?"

"When I'm in the neighborhood," Mr. Ames admitted agreeably. "Nice peaceful place to stop and eat my lunch. Or to have a snack." He ate another section of orange and dropped more peel.

"Did you ever see anyone around here before the house burned?" David asked.

"Like a tramp, you mean?" Mr. Ames sounded thoughtful.

"That's what he means," Larry said quickly. Maybe Mr. Ames was the witness who told the police he'd seen a boy there. He wished he knew for sure who it was.

"Once or twice I've seen one," Mr. Ames answered. "Mostly, I see kids fooling around in the yard."

The old man's pale blue eyes seemed to stab at Larry. "Saw a boy a couple of weeks ago looked like you. But I guess you'd have been in school that day."

I'd have been in school, Larry thought, grateful Mr. Ames hadn't said Saturday. If Ames was the witness, there wasn't much to worry about. Larry hadn't missed any school since January.

But Michael Courtney wouldn't have been in school. Maybe he'd got outside and almost escaped. Larry stole a glance at David. Wasn't that the kind of proof they were after?

David only wrinkled his nose. As they looked at each other, Mr. Ames made a sudden movement with his hand. The last part of his orange sailed past Larry's ear and rolled under a pine tree.

"Break's over," said Mr. Ames. "You boys keep out of trouble. Stop racing around the countryside on those machines and stay home where you belong."

"Okay," agreed Larry and David.

As soon as the truck had backed away, Larry said, "He's a witness! He saw Michael Courtney!"

"Maybe he did and maybe he didn't," David countered. "If you ask me, he can't see ten feet in front of him. Old guys like him should wear glasses."

"He'd wear them if he needed them," Larry said. But David was probably right, as usual. They had to get better evidence than Mr. Ames's remark.

"I'll bet he's right about a tramp being around here, though," David said. "That story about kidnappers sounded good when you were telling me. I'm not so sure now."

"It couldn't have been one tramp. Remember, the table was set for two people. And even if they found coffee that was still usable, the milk and eggs had to be fresh." Larry was determined not to lose David's help. "We're going to find something that'll prove I'm right."

"How about looking in that shed at the end of the drive?" David suggested. "It's the only thing that didn't burn."

"Good idea," Larry agreed. "Maybe the kidnapper hid his car there."

They parked their motorcycles behind the pines and slipped along the drive to the shed. Because the door was open about six inches, they could peek inside.

"Something's there!" David exclaimed.

"A tractor." Larry was looking over David's shoulder. "It's an old one."

"How old, do you think?" David pulled the door open further.

"It goes back to at least 1950." Larry took a few steps inside to look more closely. "No, I'd say more like the forties. Seems in good condition, too, except it's covered with dust and cobwebs. Looks like they hold spider conventions on it."

"I'm glad I don't have to try to farm with that bucket of bolts," David said. "No cab to keep the sun off."

"But it's air conditioned," Larry told him, pointing to the open seat.

"More air than I'd want." David turned away, laughing. "Well, nothing like a clue anywhere. If they had a car, there wasn't room to park it in here. Let's go to the house."

"Wait a minute," Larry said. He stared into the

dusty shed, amazed by his own idea. "There *is* a clue."

David's eyes widened. He looked back, inspecting the shed from top to bottom. Larry had never thought he'd feel superior to David, but at that moment he did.

"Think about when I described that kitchen. It wasn't fixed up, but it was clean. So was the other room I looked in. Nobody's lived in the house for a couple of years. There should have been dust inside. And cobwebs, like in the shed. But there weren't."

"No tramp would've cleaned," David murmured, half-convinced. "A kidnapper might have."

The boys wandered toward the house. The ruins looked the same as before. Larry knelt and began to lift objects one by one. After five minutes his hands looked like they belonged to a chimneysweep. David plunged into the mess, too, diving for a chunk of silver.

"Hey, part of the loot," he said, holding it up.

Larry laughed and took the melted mass in his hand. "Maybe part of a spoon," he said.

He gave it back, and David sent the chunk spinning down into the ruins. It crashed into something dark and delicate that might have been paper. The object crumpled and wasn't there any longer.

Larry stretched to reach the remains of a frying pan. He sat back on his heels, holding it in front of him. Could this be the same pan that had held the eggs? Now nobody would ever believe he'd seen those scrambled eggs.

David wandered around the foundation. "Look," he cried. "My footprints! I can recognize the pattern from the soles of my shoes."

Larry dropped the frying pan and went to see. "The others must be mine."

He examined the hardened ground. The last rain had been Friday night. The places where they'd walked on Saturday were easily identified. There were also the clear marks of one more pair of shoes.

"How about that?" Larry pointed to them. "Some other person walked here about the same time we did."

"Only a kid," David said. "The prints are smaller than ours."

"A kid might not be hard to find—there aren't many houses around here. Let's ride down the road again and see if we can spot him. If he hangs around here a lot, maybe he can tell us something."

"You think this guy is going to be sitting by the road waiting to talk to us?" David asked scornfully.

Larry winced. David was right again.

"There is one place we could try, though," David continued. "Remember that farmhouse where we saw the broken bicycle? A kid without wheels could be a kid who'd walk over here once in a while. I guess it wouldn't hurt to see."

"Let's go," Larry said. He was eager to leave before David changed his mind.

A bushy tree in the front yard of the white farmhouse had burst into sweet-smelling pink blossoms. The brown dog they'd seen before was sitting near it, acting as if he were guarding it. As soon as the dog saw the boys, he bounded forward, barking. They stopped and turned off their engines, hoping that would quiet him.

"Hey, dog," Larry called in the voice he used to show strange animals he was friendly. "We won't hurt you. We just want to see if anybody's home."

The dog came forward slowly, wagging his plumy tail. He continued barking, but with less enthusiasm. He obviously wanted to be petted.

A small figure wearing shorts and a sleeveless blouse crawled out from behind the bushy tree and came toward them, too. "Fine watchdog he is," said a disgusted girl's voice. "What do you guys want?"

"Are you the kid who walked around the Hartley house last Saturday?" Larry held his breath as he waited for her answer. He knew the chance of finding the right person was slim. They needed a lot of luck.

"What if I did?" The girl's small face became fierce. Maybe the dog wouldn't bite, but the girl looked as if she might.

"We wondered if you saw anybody around there just before the fire," David said, impatient as always. He pulled something from his pocket. "Give you a quarter if you'll tell us what you know."

The girl bent to quiet the dog. She was about nine years old, with dark brown hair cut short. Her eyes kept sneaking toward the money and darting away again. Finally, she held out her hand.

"Tell us first," David insisted.

"Not much to tell." She looked at the ground, clasping and unclasping her hands. "Mr. Hartley was a nice old man. The neighbors kind of looked after him before he died. His house was empty a long time. Then those people moved in down the road. They went to Mr. Hartley's house sometimes."

"Do you mean the Pilchers? Did they go inside?" Larry asked.

The girl kept looking at the dog, as if he'd tell her the answer. "I think so."

"When was the last time you saw somebody there?"

The girl's eyes had a secret look, and she didn't answer. David wiggled the quarter.

"I saw a boy near the side door a couple of weeks ago."

Larry stiffened, but she didn't say the boy looked like him.

"How about the last few days?" David asked. "Since the fire?"

"When we drove past last night after dinner, I saw the Pilchers' truck there."

"That's it? That's all you know?"

The girl nodded, watching David's hand expectantly. He gave her the quarter. As soon as she had the money, she ran away. Her dog followed, jumping at her again.

"Mrs. Pilcher's in on it, I'll bet," Larry breathed. "There were two kidnappers, Mr. Pilcher and his wife."

"Sure sounds like it," David agreed.

"Then what are we going to do?"

"I'll think of something," David said.

They headed for home, riding back past the burned house. Beyond it they passed the fields with their bursting plants. Along the side of the road up ahead was a green-and-white truck. When they came closer, Larry could see the truck's hood was up. A small figure in jeans and a faded green shirt stood dejectedly beside it.

At the sound of their motorcycles, the person turned around, and Larry saw a woman with dark hair streaked with blonde. She had to be Mrs. Pilcher. Who else in town had hair like that?

David recognized her, too. "Let's speed up. We don't want anything to do with that lady. If she tells her old man she saw us out here, he'll know we were at the house again. Then we're in trouble."

10. Rescuing Mrs. Pilcher

It wasn't easy to ignore Mrs. Pilcher. She fluttered her hand weakly and stepped directly in front of the motorcycles. They had to stop, or they would have run her down.

"You boys know anything about trucks?" She spoke so softly Larry could hardly hear her over the rumble of the motors. Coping with the stalled truck seemed to have drained all her energy. Her two-color hair dropped into her face and over her sagging shoulders, and her pale green shirt made her look like a split pea.

Larry felt sorry for her. "I'll take a look, Mrs. Pilcher. What's wrong?"

The woman shook her head. "It just stopped going, and I coasted over to the side of the road."

"Do you have gas?" asked the practical David.

Mrs. Pilcher didn't seem to hear him. "I don't know why it has to be so hot this early in the year." She fanned herself with a folded paper. "Seems more like July than the first of May. I was in a dreadful traffic jam downtown. There was some kind of accident, and everything was blocked up, and it was so hot."

She sighed loudly and turned to David. "Gas, did you say? I thought I had enough. But the engine did act kind of starving to death."

"Do you mind if I get in and check a few things?" Larry asked. He suspected David was right about the gas.

"I guess you can." Mrs. Pilcher nodded vaguely. "If you're sure you know what you're doing."

Larry opened the door and climbed inside the truck. It was fun to sit so high above the ground. For a moment he forgot why he was there. Then he remembered and looked at the dashboard.

The key was in the ignition, so he turned it. There was a whir, but the motor didn't turn over. He checked the gas gauge. According to the indicator, the tank was half-full. He tried the engine again, but nothing happened.

She'd mentioned being stuck in traffic, and the weather *was* awfully hot. Maybe there was air in the fuel line. That was what he should look for next.

Climbing out, Larry noticed a bulging sunshine-yellow cloth pouch in the passenger seat. It was probably Mrs. Pilcher's purse. Beside the purse was a dark yellow jacket. But what held his attention was a blue flight bag with the zipper on one end ripped away from the fabric.

Larry stared at the bag. A blue flight bag like that had been in the Hartley house. This bag was ripped in exactly the same place as the other one. Only it couldn't be the same bag. That one would have burned up in the fire.

He glanced up to see Mrs. Pilcher and David waiting expectantly. With an apologetic shrug, he scrambled from the truck and began to examine the engine.

"I have an idea what's wrong," he told Mrs. Pilcher. "Do you have any tools?"

"My husband has a box behind the seat. I don't know what's in it." Mrs. Pilcher's anxious brown eyes shifted from Larry to the motor and back.

"Maybe I should call him," she said. "But if I do, he'll be upset about being disturbed at work. He was just out of town on business for two weeks. He says he has a lot to catch up on."

"I won't hurt anything," Larry promised her.

"Okay, go ahead. What have I got to lose?" she asked with a grin.

Larry winked and climbed back into the cab. The toolbox was where she said it was, and he took out what he needed.

"What're you going to do?" David asked.

As he went to work on the fuel line, Larry explained. He thought David understood when he pointed to parts of the engine as he worked on them. Mrs. Pilcher didn't seem to know what he was talking about, but she watched and nodded her head as if she did.

The job took only a few minutes. Then Larry got into the driver's seat to try the motor again. If it didn't work, he wasn't sure what to try next.

He turned the key, and the engine sputtered and groaned. Then it began to run smoothly.

"You did it!" David sounded surprised. But he told Mrs. Pilcher, "Larry is really good with machinery. He can fix almost anything."

"Oh, I'm most grateful." Mrs. Pilcher looked less tired and a lot more friendly. "My Ned doesn't know one thing about cars. He hates it when they go wrong. You wouldn't think he'd be so good with houses either, but—"

Not listening to the rest, Larry leaned behind the seat to put the tools away. He jumped down to the road, and Mrs. Pilcher thanked him again. She didn't pay much attention to David, and for once David didn't try to grab the spotlight. Larry enjoyed a sense of accomplishment he didn't often feel.

"I noticed your flight bag," he began bravely. He

had just rescued Mrs. Pilcher—why should he be afraid of her? "Do you know where I could get one like it?"

"I'd give you this one if I could," she said in her soft voice. "But it belongs to my husband. I just borrowed it to carry some recipes to my cousin. She's making a cookbook, and I collected a heap of them from magazines and papers."

"I guess your husband had that bag with him when he went on his trip." Larry was afraid he'd said too much, because her eyes widened with surprise at his question.

"Oh, no," Mrs. Pilcher said quickly, "he didn't have it." She seemed to decide that her answer wasn't good enough and added, "Ned doesn't use that bag on long trips. Just the short ones. A friend of ours borrowed it while he was gone."

Sure, he did, Larry thought. He noticed she didn't name the friend, and he was certain she was lying. Mrs. Pilcher knew the bag had been used to hold ransom money. That was why she had to make up the story about someone borrowing the bag.

"Well, thanks again." Mrs. Pilcher hopped into the truck. The motor was still running, and she pulled away with a jerk.

"What was that all about?" David demanded.

"Why were you asking about some old flight bag?"

"She had a bag on the seat of the truck. I'm sure it was the one I saw in the Hartley kitchen."

"It couldn't be," David objected. "If it had been there, it'd be a cinder now."

"That's what I was thinking," Larry agreed. "But if it's the same bag and it's not burned, what does that mean?"

David stared at him, eyes narrowed, as he thought the problem through for himself. "You mean, someone took it away from the house after you saw it Saturday afternoon?"

A nod was Larry's only answer.

David thought some more. "The person who took away the bag must have been the one who torched the house. Did she really loan it to a friend?"

"No," Larry answered. "I don't think she did."

"Neither do I," David agreed. "The Pilchers must have set the fire. If they figure out you saw the flight bag in the house, you're in big trouble. You shouldn't have said a word about it to Mrs. Pilcher."

Silently, they remounted their bikes. Larry hadn't thought he could be any more scared than he'd been the last few days. Now he knew he could. He was pretty sure David was badly frightened, too.

11. Breakthrough

They decided to meet the next day, Wednesday, after school to talk about what they'd do next. Larry hated to wait, but he didn't have much choice.

Even from the beginning, Wednesday went wrong. First period he got back an English test he was sure he'd passed. As soon as he saw he hadn't, he wadded the paper and stuffed it into his pocket.

Next, he got into an argument with Stuart because he wouldn't go over to Stuart's house after school and wouldn't say why. And Stuart was getting mad because Larry had never explained more about the fire and the kidnapping.

Last, he found David had his regular appointment at the orthodontist that afternoon. David left right after school, and they didn't have a minute to talk.

Frustrated, Larry stomped home. His mother was at a meeting and Linda, who was supposed to be staying with the neighbor, sat on the kitchen floor eating a sandwich.

"What are you doing?" Larry demanded.

"I was hungry, so I came home. Mom hard-boiled eggs this morning, and I made them into egg salad all by myself. Rani helped." Linda patted the very thin black-and-white cat beside her.

Egg squeezed from between the slices of bread and plopped onto the floor. Rani's pink tongue darted out to taste, but then she turned away.

"Isn't that cat eating yet?"

"She'll eat just one thing," Linda said. "Dry cat food with brewer's yeast on it. That's a funny brown powder. I wouldn't eat it, but I guess it tastes like water buffalo to Rani."

Larry looked around his mother's usually spotless kitchen. Bread crumbs, pieces of egg, and globs of mayonnaise covered the counter.

"How did you make such a mess?" he roared. "Get back to Mrs. Barnwell's. I'll clean this up before Mom sees."

"Making egg salad is very hard," Linda explained. She stuffed the rest of her sandwich in her mouth and scooped up Rani. She danced away, squeezing the cat against her. "You're a good brother, Larry."

Well, at least one person appreciated him. Larry grabbed a handful of paper towels and attacked the counter and the floor. His mother would have made Linda do it, but he knew Linda would take forever and, in the end, he'd have to finish anyway. He dumped the soggy mass into the wastepaper basket.

Then he called Stuart and offered to come over after all. Since Stuart knew about the kidnapping, why not tell him the rest of the mystery? He'd be more help than David. Stuart was nice about inviting him again, but said that two other guys were already there. Larry decided to stay home.

Grabbing a bag of potato chips, he flopped onto the couch in the family room and thought about the kidnapping. It looked as if Mr. Pilcher had pretended to take a business trip, but went to the Hartley house instead. He used the blue flight bag to carry ransom money. When he burned the house, he took the bag away with him.

What were the other clues? Food had been set out for two people. Pants and a shirt had been dropped on the floor. *Somewhere* at the house there had to be an answer. Something out there must prove what Larry knew had happened.

That evening, just before he went upstairs to do his homework, Larry remembered the English exam in his pocket. He went into the kitchen and tore it into tiny bits, which he tucked under Linda's egg-salad garbage. He knew it was time to tell his parents he was failing English, but he didn't want to be yelled at or punished. Maybe he'd pass the next test and everything would still be okay.

On his way to his room, thinking of the Hartley house, he had an idea. It was such an incredible idea that he couldn't believe *he*'d thought of it. The terrible day had turned in an instant into a good one.

The answer to the mystery was so obvious! Why hadn't he thought of it long ago? Whistling cheerfully to himself, Larry plunged into his homework.

As soon as school was out on Thursday, he rushed home to change his clothes. David was supposed to meet him by the garage, ready to ride. The day was perfect, although dark clouds were bunching in the western sky. Wait until David heard his fantastic idea!

When Larry ran outside, ready to go, David was waiting in the Wallaces' driveway. "Come on!" Larry yelled.

The roar of a car inside the garage interrupted him. David's mother backed out, honking the horn. David closed the garage door and got into the car. It wasn't until then that Larry noticed David was still wearing his school clothes.

"Where are you going?" he bellowed.

"Shopping." David made a horrible face as he leaned out the open window. "She says we can't wait. It has to be today. I said I had plenty of clothes. So does she. But she says this is the afternoon she planned on shopping for summer things. We have to go."

Larry was furious. This couldn't be happening. David wouldn't let him down again.

"Looks like rain, so maybe it's good we can't go." David pointed at the clouds. "But we can go back tomorrow or next week or—"

Or never, Larry thought. Mrs. Wallace was backing up again even though David was still talking. The car reached the street, and Larry couldn't hear the rest of his sentence. He stood where he was, kicking at the gravel with his toe.

David had no intention of going back to the house. He just didn't want to look like a coward by saying he didn't want to go. He probably wouldn't go with Larry to talk to Officer Foreman, either.

In a way, Larry didn't blame him. He wouldn't want to go back himself if he hadn't had that wonderful idea. He couldn't stand never knowing if he was right. The proof he had in mind would be practically in plain sight. He couldn't wait around until Mr. Pilcher thought of the same thing he had and got rid of the evidence.

Larry wheeled his motorcycle out of the garage and started the engine. No matter what might happen to him, he had to visit the Hartley house that afternoon. There was no other way.

12. Dangerous Discovery

The ride to the house didn't seem as long as usual. Larry arrived well before he'd built up his courage. His stomach felt like someone was riding a motorcycle inside it. Maybe he was getting the flu and ought to go straight home.

But he knew he wasn't getting the flu.

He parked his bike and walked toward the house. After four steps, he went back to the bike and turned it around to face the street. It wouldn't hurt to be prepared to get away fast in case of trouble.

As he walked along the drive again, it seemed as if his steps crashed like thunder. Anyone within five miles would know he was there. When a bird flew past his shoulder he started as if it were a bullet and peered around suspiciously.

Nothing was going to happen just because he was there alone, Larry told himself sternly. Without David, it only *seemed* more scary. He'd come alone the first time and survived.

Remembering David's comments about rain, he looked overhead. The sky had grown gray and overcast. Maybe he *should* go home. He didn't want to get his bike soaked.

No, he couldn't leave. He'd come to look for something, and he was going to stay until he found it. A little water wouldn't hurt him or the bike. And if he had to escape for some reason, the motorcycle was ready to get him away quickly.

Of course, he wouldn't need to escape. Everything was going to work out exactly as he'd planned—and he wasn't planning on any trouble.

Larry stepped onto the small square of cement that had been the side porch and turned to face the shed. A short, overgrown path led there from the house. Larry started along the path, pretending he had a bag of garbage he wanted to throw out.

Eggshells were what he'd thought of when he had seen Linda's garbage and had the wonderful idea at home. Scrambled eggs meant eggshells, but the kitchen of the deserted house had been clean. There were no eggshells. If the garbage had been taken outside before the eggs were cooked, the shells might still exist.

Eggshells were the kind of evidence that would interest the police. If the police saw them, they might believe somebody had been staying at the house. Then they'd want to know who it was. They'd forget about blaming the owner of the red helmet for the fire.

A stand of gloriously healthy weeds had shot up beside the shed. They nearly covered a fallen, blackened object.

Larry paused. A car was coming. An instant later, he recognized the Pilchers' truck, and he dived flat on his face into the weeds. Holding his breath, he listened and waited. The truck passed.

Had the driver noticed him? Larry didn't think so. He lay still, heart thudding, but the truck didn't come back. At last he raised himself on his hands and knees and crawled over to the fire-blasted metal can.

Although the container had been tipped on its side, the cover was still on. Hardly daring to hope, Larry set the can upright.

When he took off the lid, all he could see was a piece of wadded newspaper. Then he took a breath, and the rotten smell of spoiled food billowed around him.

Larry removed the wad and plucked at the crumpled sheets. Inside were the eggshells—ten halves, plus tiny pieces. Mixed among them were coffee grounds, a milk-bottle top, and peelings from an orange.

Tremendously relieved, Larry sat back on his heels. He took time to look at the newspaper. It was a front page from a paper published in a small town about a hundred miles from Meadowvale. On the right-hand side, a headline said "Blaine Escapes Prison Farm." Under the words was a picture of a thin-faced boy with stringy, dark hair.

Something about the face was familiar. Larry stared at it until he realized it was similar to his own. If you were in a hurry, you might think the guy looked like he did. Only the face was more a man's than a boy's. Blaine must be nearly ten years older than he was.

He stared at the caption beneath the picture. It read: "Jack Blaine, Escaped Convict."

Jack Blaine was a prisoner who'd got away.

A drop of water splashed right on the picture. Startled, Larry looked up. Two more drops fell into his face. The rain was starting. His ride home was going to be long and wet, but he had what he needed.

Larry hastily wrapped the papers over the garbage again. If Mr. Pilcher realized this evidence still existed, he'd come to destroy it. Now that Larry had it in his hands, he wanted to take it directly to Officer Foreman. But how could he take it with him?

Before he could decide, the crunch of tires on the drive made him stiffen with horror. A truck rolled slowly toward him.

Immediately, he relaxed. It wasn't the green-and-white truck. It was the small tan carpenter's truck. Mr. Ames must be there to eat his afternoon snack.

Kicking the garbage can back into the cover of the weeds, Larry ran head-down to his motorcycle. He dropped the wadded newspaper into his helmet, intending to let the helmet hang from the handlebars. But as the rain fell faster, he jammed the helmet on his head.

The helmet didn't fit properly, but Larry managed to fasten the strap anyhow. Inside, the garbage scratched at his head and made crinkling sounds in his ears.

Mr. Ames stopped his truck and rolled down the window. "You're going to get soaked, boy. Climb in here with me, and I'll take you home."

"Thanks, I'm okay," Larry said. Between the raindrops and the rattle of the newspaper, he could hardly hear. He didn't want to waste time on conversation with the old man, anyway.

His discovery made him feel very protective. Nobody was going to see that evidence until he delivered it to the police station. Much as he might like a ride, he wasn't going to take any chances.

"Don't be silly." A harsher note entered into Mr. Ames's voice. He stepped out of the truck and came toward Larry.

His walk had an elastic spring, like that of a younger man. For the first time Larry noted the knotted muscles in Mr. Ames's forearms under the rolled-up sleeves of his shirt.

"Did I see you put a newspaper from the garbage in your helmet?" Mr. Ames asked. "What'd you do that for? Looks pretty uncomfortable the way it's perched on your head."

"It's okay," Larry muttered. His voice quivered, and his hands started to shake so badly he could hardly start the motorcycle.

The carpenter reached out to him with bony fingers that seemed strong and menacing. Larry ducked away from the grasping hand and zoomed off as fast as he could. The end of the driveway came so quickly that his rear tire skidded onto the road when he turned.

As he reached the first cornfield, the truck roared out of the Hartley drive and started after him. A quick

glance out of the corner of his eye showed the front fender looming behind him.

Larry leaned lower over his handlebars and steered onto the trail beside the road where he was supposed to ride. The truck veered until it was headed straight at him. Then it swayed, barely staying on the blacktop and remaining just behind him.

The rain began to fall much harder, and Larry could barely see where he was going. He'd always wanted goggles. He guessed it was too late to wish he'd bought some.

The motorcycle slipped, and he almost lost his balance. The near fall frightened him. What did Mr. Ames think he was doing, following so closely? If he wasn't careful, he'd go off the road and smash into the motorcycle.

Larry decided he had to do something to save them both. He braked suddenly and turned to the side, letting the small truck careen past him.

With the road clear, he crossed it and raced down a path to the left. It was one farmers used to get their machinery into the back fields. He and David had discovered it was a shortcut to a road that ran behind the Field.

For a moment he felt better. He'd shown the old

man a couple of tricks. Then he heard the rumbling motor of the small truck behind him again.

Mr. Ames couldn't still be following! Larry slowed until he dared look around to see.

The truck bounced crazily over the path behind him.

Why would Mr. Ames want to follow him off the road? An answer came to Larry, and it wasn't very comforting. Maybe Mr. Ames knew what he'd found in the garbage and wanted to make sure that nobody ever saw the evidence. Was he such a good friend of Mr. Pilcher that he'd go that far to help him?

Setting his hands firmly on the handlebars, Larry tore along the path. He was grateful for the long hours he'd spent practicing at the Field. Even so, every muscle in his body ached from the strain. At least the truck had fallen behind him and didn't seem to be gaining. If Larry could reach the Field, he thought he could get home.

The truck gathered speed and rushed closer. To reach the road that ran behind the Field more quickly, Larry took a jump he wouldn't usually have tried. He soared through the air for what seemed a long time before his bike wheels splatted into the mud.

Larry tensed as he began to skid, but he regained

his balance and veered between two trees. Safely beyond them, he bounced onto the concrete road. The last trick confused Mr. Ames. He brought the truck to a screeching halt with its bumper resting against one of the trees. He had to back up and move slowly until he reached the tractor exit from the field.

Larry rushed down the hill above the boys' practice area. There was a bumpy path the guys from that side of the subdivision used. He flew across the familiar Field amid a muddy spray. This time he wasn't doing it for fun.

At last he made it to the short access road from the Field to the regular street. Two more blocks and he'd be home. He wondered if he could make it. His arms felt like wornout rubber bands, and he didn't have as much control over his bike as he'd had when he started out.

Even though he had to slow once he was on the glistening, wet pavement, Larry had gained half a block on the truck. For the first time he noticed he was soaking wet. Cold air rushed over him, and each drop of rain felt like a sharp, icy splinter.

Mr. Ames must have realized Larry was nearly home. In a last, desperate rush, he roared forward again. This is crazy, Larry thought. One of us is going to get killed. He skidded at the edge of a puddle and barely escaped. By the time his motorcycle was steady, the truck was in position to try again. Now he understood there was only one possible reason for this long, dangerous chase. Mr. Ames *did* want him dead.

The street was deserted except for one car parked at the corner. Larry could barely see it because the rain was coming down so hard. Water flew in every direction. He bent his head to concentrate on getting all the speed he could.

He could feel the truck near him again. He didn't dare look. It was all he could do to keep his bike upright. He was too tired to dodge when the truck charged directly at him.

13. Larry Finds the Answer

The wail of a siren sliced through the rain. At the last second, the small truck spun past Larry. Right behind it swooped the blue car that had been parked at the corner. As everyone slowed, Larry recognized the markings on the car's side.

The police car jammed itself in front of the truck to force it over to the side of the road. Larry pulled up beside the car, taking great gulps of air. He felt as if he'd been riding forever. The bike was too heavy to balance between his wobbly legs, and he let it fall to the pavement.

Officer Foreman jumped out of his car, leaving the motor running. He ran to the driver's side of the truck and yanked the door open.

Good old Officer Foreman! Larry thought. He'd never again resent the policeman because he always parked near the Field. If it hadn't become his regular stopping place, he wouldn't have been there when Larry needed him.

Unsure what to do, Larry waited where he was. He knew only one thing: he wouldn't leave until he'd told Officer Foreman everything he knew about the Hartley house. His evidence was still safe and dry inside his helmet. It was the only thing about him that was dry.

As the rain subsided to gentle tapping, Mr. Ames staggered down from the truck. His shoulders drooped, and Larry was surprised to realize the chase had also been exhausting for the elderly man.

"You were driving recklessly, sir," Officer Foreman said. "When I looked up from my radio I saw you nearly swerve into the motorcycle."

"I'm afraid the lad's a bit excited," Mr. Ames said. "We were talking, and suddenly he up and raced away from me. I didn't know what to think, so I followed him. Guess the rain made him careless. But I couldn't help it that he drove his machine right in front of my truck."

Officer Foreman turned to Larry. "You *were* riding in the road. And you know that's against the law. We're going to have to—"

"Wait!" Larry cried. "Look at this. Please!"

He jerked off his helmet and held out the smelly, wadded newspaper. The raindrops in his hair felt good. For once he could see his mother's point about feeling better when you were clean. His head felt crawly, as if he might never be able to scrub it back to the way it had been before.

Looking uncertain, the policeman accepted the flattened wad and began to unfold it.

"Careful, don't lose the eggshells," Larry warned. "They're evidence. I found them at the Hartley house. Somebody was using it before it burned. I went inside that day and I saw."

The policeman looked down his nose. He held the bundle of newspaper at an uncomfortable arm's length. Raindrops splashed upon it one by one.

"I'm a busy man," interrupted Mr. Ames. "Give me a ticket if you have to, and I'll leave you to take care of the boy. Just drop that garbage in the back of my truck. I'll get rid of it for you."

Officer Foreman looked at him understandingly. He moved his arm as if he were about to toss away Larry's evidence. A piece of moldy orange peel dropped out of the newspaper to the pavement.

Larry felt as if the whole world were falling with it. Orange peel! Mr. Ames was the person who was always eating oranges. That was why he wanted Larry's evidence so badly he would have killed him. He wasn't doing any favor for the Pilchers by catching Larry. Mr. Ames was the person who'd used the Hartley house!

"He burned down the Hartley house!" Larry blurted. His stomach was loop-the-looping, but he kept on talking. "He found the broken window and knew someone had been inside the house. He wanted to make sure nobody else saw the things he'd left there. I'll bet he's the one who borrowed the flight bag. Talk to Mrs. Pilcher."

He could have said a lot more, but he was beginning to shiver. His teeth chattered so loudly he could hardly talk.

"I think you'd better go home," Officer Foreman told him. He was frowning, but he didn't throw the evidence away. He put it carefully in his car, and his eyes never left Mr. Ames. The policeman's muscles rippled under his jacket as if he expected the carpenter to try to escape.

Mr. Ames was poised on the balls of his feet. He looked ready to run, but he didn't move.

"This man and I are going to the station for a little talk," the policeman continued. "Stay home till I come by. Then I'm going to want a discussion with you and your parents."

During the next hours Larry felt as if he'd fallen into the middle of a detective movie. A policeman came to the house and talked to his mother. After Larry showered and changed into dry clothes, they all went to the station, where his father met them. There they talked to more policemen. Larry had to tell them everything he'd done, alone or with David.

It was nearly dark when Larry and his parents got home. Although the evening was cold and damp, David was sitting on the Wallace front steps. As soon as he saw the car, he dashed over.

"Why didn't you wait for me? I heard what happened on the radio. Now you're a hero, and I'm not!"

"If I'd known how it was going to be, I wouldn't have gone! Never!" Larry still felt shaky when he thought about what had happened.

"Were the Pilchers kidnappers after all?" David's eyes sparkled with excitement and envy. "Did they really try to kill you to keep you from talking?"

Larry's parents walked across the street to get his sister from Mrs. Barnwell, who was watching her. The boys went into Larry's family room and sat on the couch.

"It wasn't quite how I figured it." Larry paused, not sure how to explain.

David looked disappointed. "Then what *did* happen?"

"Mr. Pilcher went out of town on a business trip for two weeks, just like we heard," Larry said. "His wife stayed home working on their house. They fix up houses and sell them. They had a key for the Hartley house because they were thinking of buying it."

"I don't understand," David said.

"Mr. Ames's grandson, Jack Blaine, was in a state prison. He was sent there after he shot a man in a holdup. I saw clippings about the Blaine trial when I was at the house, but it was hard for me to read them, so I didn't."

"If I'd been there, I would have read them and there wouldn't have been any mystery," David boasted.

"I paid more attention to the money," Larry admitted.

"The piece of a hundred-dollar bill." David nodded.

"Anyway, the grandson escaped from prison, and Mr. Ames helped him hide in the Hartley house. He stole the key from the Pilchers and copied it. And he gave the grandson all the money he had so Jack could start a new life. He borrowed the flight bag from Mrs. Pilcher to carry it from the bank. It wasn't ransom money I saw—it was escape money."

"An escaped convict!" David was definitely impressed.

"Jack Blaine hid at the house for nearly a week. That was why Mr. Ames cleaned the kitchen and the next room. He kept the kitchen neat, but the grandson dropped his prison clothes on the floor in the other room and never touched them again. He just sat around watching television. The curtains were closed so nobody would see him."

"Somebody did, though," David interrupted. "Who was that witness Foreman talked about?"

"That was the neighbor girl we found. Maybe Jack went outside for a minute with the garbage. Ames brought plenty of food and ate some meals with him. Jack drank a lot of milk because he couldn't get all he wanted in prison."

"Was there really a telephone?" David wanted to know. "You weren't imagining that, were you? You did hear a phone ring?"

"Mr. Ames had a phone installed so Jack could arrange a ride to Mexico with a friend. The police found the worker who installed it, and he identified Mr.

Ames. Mr. Ames told the phone company he was renting the house."

"That was a tricky thing to do." David pulled a daffodil out of a vase on the coffee table.

"The minute the friend came, Jack ran out," Larry explained. "He didn't even wait to eat the supper he'd cooked or say good-bye to his grandfather."

"Blaine sounds rotten to me," David said. "I'm glad we didn't run into him."

"Me, too," Larry agreed. "Anyway, after Jack Blaine left, Mr. Ames was going to clear everything away so no one would ever know they'd used the Hartley house. But when Mr. Ames came Saturday night, he saw the broken window and my dollar bill. He got scared and decided he had to burn the house. Then nobody could ever connect it with Jack Blaine."

David was picking the petals off the flower one by one. He let them drop on the floor like a pile of gold coins. "If you hadn't gone inside that afternoon, nobody would ever have known."

Eyes wide, Larry nodded.

The doorbell rang, and they both jumped to their feet.

"Who's that?" David asked. "Your mom and dad?"

"They wouldn't ring the bell," Larry said. "I guess I'd better answer it. You come with me."

They opened the door to Mr. and Mrs. Pilcher.

"Evening." Mr. Pilcher smiled until his eyes narrowed so the blue hardly showed.

Mrs. Pilcher grinned as if they were old friends.

"Hi," Larry said, feeling strange. They weren't kidnappers after all. Did they know he'd suspected them?

"We've been to see Ames," Mr. Pilcher told them. "I feel a bit responsible for what happened because we were trusted with the key to the Hartley house. We never suspected Ames took it and made a copy."

Larry and David stood in the hall with the door open. Neither thought to invite the Pilchers inside.

"We're not the only ones at fault, though." Mr. Pilcher didn't seem to mind talking from the porch. "I want to point out that you boys have some responsibility for what happened. You shouldn't have gone into the house."

"I didn't do it," David interrupted. "I didn't go in. It was Larry. He went in."

Mr. Pilcher looked stern. "You should have talked to an adult as soon as you found someone had been using the house. Blaine might have been caught, and old Mr. Ames wouldn't be in such a pickle that he'll probably go to prison himself. I'm sorry to say he wanted to kill you, Larry. Now it's over he knows he was wrong, and he's sorry. He got too excited trying to get the evidence you found."

With a loud sigh Mr. Pilcher wiped the back of his big hand across his bald head. "Okay, that's what I thought I should say to you."

"Was Mr. Ames the person who borrowed your airline bag?" Larry asked.

Mrs. Pilcher smiled and nodded.

"One more thing." Mr. Pilcher scratched his head. "Hear you're pretty handy, Larry. Bonnie and I thought you might do some work for us this summer. We have a house near you we're going to be repairing. Boy like you could help us a lot. I intended to ask if you could work last Saturday when I invited you into our house, but you were as jumpy as a fox in a henhouse. Even drove down later that day to the field where you boys ride, hoping to talk to you again. Well, I could see you were too busy then."

"That's why you were at the Field?" Larry asked. "What about the library on Monday? Why were you there?"

"Oh, Bonnie and I've been reading their books

on home repairs. I stopped to get some new ones because I had extra time after a meeting that ended early. Didn't think you saw me. You and your friend seemed in a big hurry."

"We were," Larry said, ashamed to admit why they'd left so fast.

"Well, you think about working for me," said Mr. Pilcher. "We'll talk more later."

"You forgot to tell him he could pick up his helmet at the station," Mrs. Pilcher said as they left. "They won't need it now."

"What a bunch of beans," David scoffed almost before the door closed. " 'You boys have some responsibility for what happened. You should have talked to an adult.' " He poked the bare stem of the daffodil between his teeth.

"Mr. Pilcher was just trying to help," Larry replied. "And I think maybe he was right. Sometimes you have to tell."

Now that it was too late, he could see what he should have done. And he could see he had another problem that was going to get him into trouble if he didn't say something. He had to let his parents know he was failing English.

Later, while Larry and his parents ate a late supper

of pizza with olives and extra cheese, he told them. His mother and father weren't as mad as he'd expected. And after his mother took him to the eye doctor on Friday afternoon, they even felt sorry for him because there was a reason for his reading problem.

"What do you mean, something's wrong with your eyes?" David roared when he heard.

They were in David's front yard, and the two mothers were talking nearby.

"It's not ordinary eye trouble. Regular check-ups didn't catch it. It's more that the eyes and the brain don't work together the way they should. I've always had trouble reading, and I thought it was because I was dumb. But they said if I wasn't pretty smart, I would have failed something years before now. A lot of intelligent people have my problem. I had lots of tests to help them understand exactly what's wrong."

"You're so good with machines and that stuff," David said. "I just figured you weren't interested in wasting your time with studying."

"I'm going to repeat my English class this summer with a tutor," Larry said. "They think I can catch up before high school starts. Maybe I'll get to tape-record classes so I can listen to them later and learn that way."

"Not bad," David said, impressed.

"Stuart's going to help me, too. And I'm going to work for the Pilchers. Stuart will be doing that with me sometimes."

"He will?" For a moment David looked surprised, but he recovered so fast Larry wasn't certain. "I'm going to be pretty busy myself. I figure I'll find another mystery to solve. I would have figured out what was going on at the Hartley house if I hadn't had to go to the orthodontist and shopping."

"No more mysteries," David's mother said, coming over to them. "And you're not going to risk your life the way Larry did. That motorcycle of yours is going up for sale this weekend."

"I knew you were going to say that!" David was outraged. "I knew that house was going to get me in trouble. But I stayed away. You can't dump my bike."

"Oh, yes, I can." His mother headed for their house with David right behind, arguing all the way.

"I guess you'll want me to sell my bike, too, after what happened," Larry said to his mother.

"What do you think?" she asked.

To his surprise, he realized he wouldn't be that upset if he lost his bike. "I guess I could do without it. I'm going to be with Stuart a lot this summer, and he doesn't have one. I'll probably be too busy working for Mr. Pilcher to do much riding, anyway."

"Have I told you your dad and I are very proud of you?" His mother put an arm around his shoulders. "You made a lot of mistakes, but you were determined and you used your head. I think you're growing up."

Larry looked down at her, hardly believing what she was saying. His parents didn't praise him very often. To his amazement, he realized he *was* looking down. "Hey, you're right. I'm taller than you are. I *am* grown up."

Mrs. Kenniston laughed, and after a moment, so did Larry.

"Will you help me write an ad for the bike?" he asked. "I can get it in next week's paper."

"Are you sure?"

"I'm sure," Larry answered. And he was.